London Burns

Tales from the world of ADRIAN'S UNDEAD DIARY

Volume Two

Chris Philbrook

London Burns: Tales from the world of Adrian's Undead Diary, Volume 1

Published in the United States of America

First Publishing Date 2016

Cover design and interior layout by Alan MacRaffen

www.macraffen.com

Also by Chris Philbrook:

Elmoryn - The Kinless Trilogy
Book One: Wrath of the Orphans
Book Two: The Motive for Massacre
Book Three: The Echoes of Sin

Reemergence
Tesser: A Dragon Among Us
Ambryn: The Cheaters of Death

Adrian's Undead Diary
Book One: Dark Recollections
Book Two: Alone No More
Book Three: Midnight
Book Four: The Failed Coward
Book Five: Wrath
Book Six: In the Arms of Family
Book Seven: The Trinity
Book Eight: Cassie

A.U.D. Anthology
Unhappy Endings: Tales from the World of Adrian's Undead Diary
London Burns: Tales from the World of Adrian's Undead Diary

Short Fiction:
Colony Lost: The Children of Ghara
Coming Soon:
Colony Lost: Book One

*Don't miss Chris Philbrook's **free** e-Book:*
At Least He's Not On Fire:
A Tour of the Things That Escape My Head

TABLE OF CONTENTS:

London Burns

Part One - The Warden Moves 7

Part Two - For Queen and Country, but Mostly the Guy Next to Me 25

Part Three - The Last Few Steps 37

Roots Grown Deep

An Elmoryn Short Story 43

About the Author 63

Additional Online Content 64

- Part One -

The Warden Moves

June 23rd, 2010

"What's the gig, Sergeant?" Harold Parker asked his squad leader over the roar of noise. The men could only hear each other over the thudding rotors hammering the air of the Lynx helicopter they rode in due to the thick headsets they wore. Communication cables connected them to the ceiling of the chopper and allowed for those traveling to and from war to speak to one another. These men weren't headed to war, at least not in the traditional sense they could've expected.

Sergeant Beck looked out the window of the helicopter as they flew in a low, wide arc around the crowded airspace of Heathrow airport. Planes on the ground below were backed up three and four deep on every runway and the planes above circled impatiently, waiting to land as their fuel supplies dwindled lower and lower. The airport looked just as bad as the roads leading to and from it with the traffic and accidents.

The Royal Marines had watched on televisions back at their base as panic set in with the word of the dead rising on foreign lands. Martial Law had been declared in a dozen countries to try and halt the spread of whatever illness was causing people to attack one another, and as the rumors on the flickering telly had it, come back from the dead. The Marines were peeled away from their ready room in Taunton by the call to go to work. The spectacle on television was replaced by the one slipping by below as they flew to Heathrow airport. It seemed as if every citizen in the United Kingdom had been struck with lunacy at the thought of the undead being real and the general public exhibited their madness through driving like bloody assholes. They'd seen a hundred accidents on the road, and nearly as many columns of smoke rising into the sky.

"An American dignitary and his bodyguards need an airlift to RAF Mildenhall. We are to hold their hand and bring the bastards there," Beck said, unimpressed with their mission and distracted by the severe worries of the day. He'd listened to the radio before they left, and the reports of widespread death and destruction in Africa and Asia cluttered his thoughts and caused great worry.

"Sarge," a lance corporal Patil said, "Do you think this shit is legit? Do you think there really are dead people coming back to life?" Patil looked at Beck with big brown eyes filled with the hope that what was happening, wasn't.

"I'm no brainiac," Beck replied. "But it seems like the dead coming back to life is a far-fetched idea, Patil. They're dead. There's no coming back from dead, you know? Now are all these crazy people acting like the end is nigh? Yeah, they are. That's a real problem. Your family have any timely legends from India about this?"

"Nothing that won't get me harassed and made fun of."

The young British Marines laughed, but they did it to hide anxiety. Evidence mounted as the morning wore on and the flight continued that made the sergeant's assertions less reasonable, and that made the men feel mad. Visible crowds fighting, building fires, drivers flying about evading other drivers. From the air, the fenced-in portion of land that was Heathrow seemed calm by comparison.

The helicopters circled, and began to land near a distant private jet hangar.

The black skinned Marine Harold sat apart from the rest of his unit, his lips pursed, his eyes fixed below on the rising earth. He held his L85 rifle pointed at the floor of the Lynx in strong hands. A small private jet had just finished taxiing below and the British chopper pilots were putting their two-chopper escort down nearby. Heavily armed men wearing khaki cargo pants, heavy button-down shirts and in most cases body armor poured out of the plane and dropped to their knees, pulling security. Hal watched a man fall to the ground in the center, blood pouring from his upper leg in a torrent, staining the slate tarmac a ruddy, wet purple.

"Problem on the ground sir," Hal said. "Looks to be one leg injury straight off the plane and a bunch of men with M-16s pulling security. They've had an incident on the plane."

Beck crawled over to the side of the plane Hal sat on and looked down at the unfolding mess. The choppers descended, and flared their noses to land.

"Those are M4s, Hal. You know that. Safeties off boys. Zombies or not, shit's going down. Act like you're one of the boys that took Umm Qasr."

"Could we do it quicker than 'em?" Hal quipped. "I've got leave starting tomorrow to help my dad with my mum's surgery. Those Iraq boys took days to unfuck themselves on that battle and I've shit to do."

Beck looked at Hal somberly and snapped his L85's safety off. "I wouldn't count on that leave, Hal."

The Marine sighed, and the chopper touched down with a bounce on the landing gear.

A second later the doors flew open and the Marines poured out onto the ground like volcanic runoff, moving in every direction and taking knees with their rifles aimed at threats that were nowhere to be found. Hal took a knee in the direction of the hangars and watched as tiny people in the airport's distance ran about, afraid for their lives. The curious or stupid stopped to watch the Marine activity, so far from the rest of the airport.

"Corporal Adamson, attend the injured man," Beck ordered. One of the Marine medics got up from his position and ran to the fallen man. His fading moans of pain were drowned out by the aural chaos of the plane's engines and chopper's beating blades.

Once the Marines were established and knew the area to be safe enough, the sergeant stood and walked toward a frightened suit-wearing man with white hair. Near him was a taller man wearing a white baseball cap with the letters WPG embroidered in black letters on the front. Tiny spatters of dried blood stood out against the white.

"Gentlemen, who is in charge here?" Beck shouted over the rotors at the suit and the hat.

"Kevin Whitten, WPG team leader. This is Senator Henke. We were under the instructions that you were to exfil us via helicopter to RAF Mildenhall for further evacuation?"

"Aye mate. How many men do you have? This everyone?" Beck shook the civilian contractor's hand firmly and watched in the corner of his eye as the suited politician scowled at the two of them. The suit looked left out and offended. This wasn't a time for politics or diplomacy. This wasn't a time for that man. The time for that man could be a very long way off, indeed.

Kevin assessed the situation. "Yeah, we lost two earlier today in Jerusalem, and we lost two more on the plane just a minute ago. This shit is horrible, brother."

Beck started to talk but he froze when he heard corporal Adamson yelp out and stumbled backwards nearby. The sergeant turned and watched as the contractor with the terrible leg injury sat up and snapped at the Marine. His fingers opened and shut reflexively—like an infant's—as his teeth gnashed. The contractor's listless eyes had gone milky white and the color of his flesh had faded to a jaundiced shade of blue-gray. The man obviously had died, yet continued to move. More evidence mounted that lunacy of the day was rooted in fact.

Over the deafening plane and the beat of the chopper's rotors Beck heard two snaps from a handgun and immediately watched as the dead man's head rocked backwards then impacted the hard tarmac below. He turned and saw Kevin holster a Glock. The American had killed his own man and he'd done it quickly. Beck examined Kevin's face and saw resolution and pain. He saw the face of a cowboy putting down his beloved horse. The man from the outskirts of Sheffield knew then and there Kevin had seen terrible things in the world that day, and had set foot on the path to the horrible changes needed to live in that world. This world. Beck felt a chill, and ignored it.

The Sergeant turned to a frightened Corporal Adamson and watched as he stood, covered in the yank's blood. They caught eyes and the younger warrior nodded. He was okay.

Beck organized the battlefield. "Americans please load up, yeah? You here, Senator and lady with you and Kevin in that bird. Hal you go with them, thank you. We are in the air in sixty seconds. Barrels down, as you know."

The local Marines guided the foreigners and they all loaded up into the cramped helicopters. True to Beck's word they lifted up within a minute's time, leaving the airplane alone on the tarmac, empty and waiting for its new passengers. A few nervous glances out of windows later they were skimming over the jammed up roads leading into London.

*****

Hal took up his position in the aft of the Lynx with his L85's barrel pressed against the hard deck of the helo and the fire selector returned to the safe position. His weapon would not discharge accidentally. Not while he had charge of it and certainly not in front of a cluster of foreigners. He'd die first.

The older man wearing the dark blue suit with the tiny American flag pin on the lapel sat beside him. Hal judged him to be either nervous or right well furious based on how the man wrung his hands together and stared at the contractor with the white baseball cap. Stared at the back of his head, more accurately. The cap wearer sat next to the blood-soaked medic Adamson. Hal thought the man said his name was Kevin. At the moment, Kevin was communicating with the pilot via headset.

Hal turned from looking out the window at the unfolding mess of metro London below to the old man. The old man noticed Hal's attention and smiled like a politician who'd spotted a camera. In truth, he looked as if he already wore the makeup for a photo-op.

"Cheers," Hal said in a yell. "Welcome to the United Kingdom is this your first visit?"

"Thank you," the suit said back equally loud. "My fifth visit actually. I wish my return was under different pretenses."

"Aye. Might I ask your name?"

"Senator Henke," he replied, extending one of his wringing hands. Hal took it in his dark hand. The politician's skin felt cool, and the shake firm. It felt practiced but not overdone.

"Corporal Harold Parker. Sorry about the sudden nature of your visit and all the mess you've dealt with. Where was your last stop?"

"Jerusalem. I was giving a speech," Henke said. Hal noted how the man's eyes glassed over from the thoughts of the day. The senator looked to the blonde woman who shook at his side in visible discomfort in the helicopter. She looked as afraid as an expensive cat thrown in a junkyard dog pen.

"Terrorists?"

"That's how it started," Henke said, staring out the window in the helicopter's door. Hal couldn't tell if the man was experiencing negative memories or if he'd turned the corporal out. A glance out the window told Hal the man probably stared at a column of oily, black smoke that rose from a house fire in western London. Judging by the thickness of the smoke it had to be a big fire.

"But that's not how it finished? Things got worse then, yeah?" Hal pressed. Information he gained now could be useful later. Even if it wasn't, talking passed the time.

"The men they shot... Wouldn't die. Never seen anything like it. Horror," Henke said. "You couldn't imagine the horror of it all. SO much blood. And the screaming..."

"Wouldn't die, or died and came back? Substantial difference, sir," Hal said with a sly smile.

Henke didn't respond to the joke. "Some of them died I think. Many, actually. Most, probably. But they got up and attacked people anyway. Biting and clawing, beating on people. Trying to kill again. Some died for good. By that I mean stayed dead. I don't know. Harold, it doesn't make sense. They acted like animals."

"Fighting rarely makes sense in my experience. But it must be done sparingly at times for the good of the people. The bloody ignorant," Hal said. "Sit tight and rest assured. You're in a perfectly good piece of aviation equipment flying over a fine nation and you are protected by multiple well-trained men with many firearms. We'll have you to your destination soon. Precious little to fret over."

"That's very reassuring Mr. Parker. Thank you for trying to make me feel more comfortable. Now if you'll excuse me, I'm going to close my eyes and try to rest."

"Absolutely, sir."

Henke closed his eyes and rested his head back. The vibration from the chopper's rotors not far above lulled the man into what looked like a deep sleep and Hal turned his attention to Adamson, who sat a few feet away, still soaked in blood. His chin rested on his chest and his head swung side to side as the helicopter rocked in flight. He seemed far too still.

"Adamson," Hal said, reaching out towards the medic. Hal couldn't see his face and the way the medic's head moved bothered him. Harold's eyes caught a pair of rips in the man's sleeve right above the wrist. The fabric had the unmistakable series of round tears that were mouth-sized. He'd been bitten.

Adamson's head rolled to the side as the helicopter gained altitude. His face finally moved to where Hal could see it. He wasn't asleep or dead. Adamson had changed. He'd become something different. The former brown corneas of Adamson's eyes had thinned in their opacity and color until they looked like tea with too much milk, sprayed with foul yellow and red flecks. His mouth hung open and his tongue explored his lips and teeth with an absence of sense and decorum. He looked like a rabid dog thirsting for water—or blood—in the desert.

The chopper suddenly bounced upward as it gained altitude again, and Adamson came out of his seat and tumbled head over heels into the opening of the cockpit. He landed head up at the shoulder of the pilot and found warm, yielding flesh presented to his mouth. He bit hard and savage below the edge of the pilot's helmet. The dog found his water.

Bright red arterial blood sprayed the ceiling panels, the controls, the windscreen and the copilot. So much came free so fast the interior of the cockpit was either bathed in blood itself, or turned red from the light shining through the blood on the glass. The quantity and force of the red blood astounded Hal but he lost his amazement as the helicopter began to spin out of control. The American contractor leapt over the consoles and gear separating the cockpit from the rest of the helicopter in the fracas and grabbed Adamson, yanking and pulling to get him off the doomed pilot. The man's heroic effort was wasted. The pilot had died, the chopper was going down, and nothing mattered.

The copilot called out mayday over and over as they plummeted downward into metropolitan London.

Hal grabbed the Senator and pinned him into the seat with all the strength he could muster, and prayed for his mother and father. With God's mercy and grace, he didn't feel the impact as the chopper smashed into the street below.

*****

The world had gone upside down. More accurately the helicopter had gone upside down. The world proper was still right-side-up, though who knew how long that would last. Everything else seemed to be well on the way to getting tossed on its head.

Hal opened his eyes and looked around inside the topsy-turvy rear compartment of the Lynx. The white capped man was moving about the upside down cabin with purpose as another member of his team snapped a broken finger back into place with a grunt and a sharp exhalation. Beyond the man named Kevin and his friend with the broken finger lay two dead men in the cockpit. The pilot had died before they'd crashed and the copilot in the other seat had been eviscerated by the front structure of the chopper during the impact. His body twitched strangely almost to the beat of the other chopper's rotors outside and above, unnerving Hal.

The old man Harold had pinned against the back of the cabin with his body had survived the crash. He had clearly been knocked upside the head with the bird getting tossed over. A clump of his gray hair was fused together by dried, sticky blood from a head wound. His eyes refused to focus as he tried to help his blonde aide.

The tall lady saw her mangled foot at the end of her calf and her breathing became ragged and imprecise. She pleaded to Kevin and Henke to help her, to give her something for the pain, but they didn't. Henke had nothing to give and Kevin simply wouldn't give her anything. You didn't give pain meds quickly in combat. The relief could trigger a drop in blood pressure that could kill.

Judging by what was happening outside the crashed helicopter the hurt people aboard the downed bird would absolutely be in combat within minutes, if not less. Hundreds were outside the helicopter injured or dead in the neighborhood they had come to ground in. The crash had caused tremendous damage, and judging by the bodies outside, numerous deaths. Some of the bodies were beyond death, in the day's new form of existence.

Hal watched in the distance of the outdoor London market they had nearly all died at and watched as the already-dead feasted on the warm flesh of the dying. He could hear the screams of his countrymen and the distant, shrill sounds of death and suffering made him shudder. He wanted to help; he needed to help but he knew he couldn't. Mission first. Hal's rifle hung on his chest, still attached by the sling. He felt relief, and readied his weapon.

One of his brothers wrenched the sliding door of the Lynx sideways, and the real world outside came in. The smell of burning fuel, soot and scorched flesh poured in and ran up Hal's nose. His nasal passages itched and burned, rebelling against the horrors his nostrils had been exposed to. The sounds grew as well; the formerly muffled screams were now loud and invasive, real and un-ignorable in a way that would scar all of them forever, should they survive the day.

Hal went into the breach with his friends once more and exited the chopper. He went again to one knee on the hard stone half a dozen paces from the flipped helicopter and assessed the situation through the 4x SUSAT optic attached to the top of his rifle. He flicked the safety to a more dangerous position.

The day's sun descended at a slower rate than the death happening below it. The men had somehow lost half an hour's time, maybe more when they crashed. Golden rays of ignorant light beamed between buildings and the cloud above were picking up edges of purple and pink as the first stages of sunset arrived. Earth and Sun did their thing above regardless of mankind's struggles below. And struggle they did.

Hundreds of men and women—many dragging children and elderly along roughly—ran and screamed as the dead tore through them. The crash of the helicopter had killed or maimed dozens in the time the passengers sat unconscious, protected by the same hull of the vehicle that killed so many on impact. A score of bodies were littered still around them. People killed by debris, the helicopter's impact, or internal injuries who had yet to reanimate. Hal felt like he sat in the middle of a minefield.

The crash victims who were shopping innocuously at London's busy Covent Garden Market were now taking up arms, fists and teeth against their shocked fellow shoppers. A horrified Harold Parker watched as three girls no older than year ten or eleven in school took a mother carrying an infant down to the hard stone of the courtyard only fifty meters distant. A smear of blood appeared on the smooth stones where the infant's head would've come into contact with the ground. He watched as they clubbed the mother with their fists and then crouched low to bite and tear into her soft flesh.

Hal put the tip of his SUSAT optic prong on the body of one of the teens and rested his finger on the trigger.

He couldn't shoot. He simply couldn't. He hadn't been

cleared to fire and even if he had, he couldn't imagine killing a teenager, even one who was dead-not-dead. Kevin hollered. Hal didn't hear who he spoke to, but he knew it wasn't to him. Somehow his brain knew.

"Marines on the ground you are clear to fire to protect yourselves or your charges," Sergeant Beck said in their ears. He rode in the chopper hovering in the air above. "Operational command on the ground is Corporal Parker. Listen to the man named Whitten if needed, Hal. God's speed."

"Roger," Hal said back to his sergeant. "You heard Beck, boys. Fire at anyone presenting danger. May God sort us out." A few rifle shots popped in response, then built to a steady vibration of constant fire. There were too many dangerous people to shoot in too little time. Hal found his strength of will and pulled the trigger on his rifle. He watched as one of the teenage girls atop the mother took his round in the chest and toppled over. He fired again at another girl before his brain could tell his fingers to stop.

The American leading the security team yelled. "Alrighty, we're following the bird to an exfil site. They are gonna put down on the Strand, 500 feet south that way!"

Hal didn't need to tell his Marines what to do. He and his two warrior-brothers stood and began to circle the wreck, heading the group south towards the main thoroughfare of London. They stepped over and around dead bodies and upended curb stones.

"Move, move! They're coming back!" Kevin yelled.

Hal looked down and saw the bodies that had been still were now moving. Their arms regained awkward movement, slowly spinning up like someone awakening after a long and deep slumber. Their eyes opened, ripened like a corpse filled with maggots and leeched of their life, love and color. The gray and yellow orbs spun, sunken in sockets, finding purpose; life to pursue and life to kill. The bloodied dead began to sit up and reach out for the Marines and men and woman they sought to protect. The three Marines formed a rough triangle shape around them as they moved.

Hal led the Senator and his aide away with his Marines as the gunfire began. His rifle bucked against his shoulder as he put accurate rounds into the chests of people who started their day with a plan that didn't include being perforated by 5.56mm NATO rounds. Hal's unit members joined him and within a moment the civilian contractors joined in as well. Above in the Lynx that didn't crash Harold could hear the pops of quieter rifle fire as his fellows supported the best they could. He envied their elevated firing position.

Hal put another round into a woman's chest as he walked slowly and watched with amused horror as she stumbled, gathered herself, and pushed forward. Near to her was woman with stellar brown hair over fair skin who sat up, dead as could be. She looked mannequin perfect if you could ignore the hole in her neck where her throat should've been. The contractor Kevin aimed carefully as he reached Hal's side and pulled his trigger, popping the woman's head and dropping her body back to the hard stone. She no longer looked perfect.

"Hit the head. Only head shots," he said with practiced calm before firing at a different dead person approaching.

Just like the movies, then. Hal knew his men were putting rounds into the chests of dangerous people, not their heads. They trained to shoot center mass, to shoot at the chest and belly. It would require an adjustment on their part…

"Head shots only men, destroy the brain!" Hall hollered to his men. They made the adjustment he expected them to and rounds began their march towards faces and foreheads. The much smaller target the skull presented meant more misses, but it also meant more kills once the rounds found their homes. The slower gait of the dead gave the men a spare second to aim, so long as they kept their distance. Proximity removed safety.

To keep distance they had to move.

Kevin scooped up the senator and his aide and helped them along, firing his rifle with the stock fully collapsed in one hand like a pistol. Somehow they man fired accurately, and in the corner of Hal's eye he saw every threat that came towards the politician and his limping secretary get dropped.

With Hal in the lead, they rounded the final corner to head directly south on a downhill street towards the Strand. Shoulder to shoulder a hundred wide and a hundred deep he saw the listless shuffle of more dead. The main thoroughfare of the city had already been filled with an army of the fallen. He hadn't expected a wall of the dead and he had no distance, and no time to aim.

Zombies didn't need to aim. They had only to grab and bite, to tackle and chew. Proximity removed danger.

Hal went down to the pavement stones on his back with the press of at least three or four bloody dead on him. He flailed hard with elbows, gloved fists, his helmet, knees and boots. Everything he had became a weapon. His rifle's hard stock smacked into the jaw of a twenty-something man who wore broken glasses. The blow jarred the spectacles off the man's face and dislocated his lower jaw nearly 90 degrees. Hal heard Kevin's weapon spray on full-auto from just a few meters away. He heard the hard smacks of rounds hitting the cement or stone above at head height. The high pitched vibrations of a skipped rounds singing through the air came soon after. He heard and felt bodies fall at his feet and the ground around him; Kevin wouldn't risk firing into the group on top of Hal, but he killed all those who tried to join.

Adrenaline surged and took over. Hal see-sawed his rifle back and forth across his chest as he felt the sudden ache of teeth sinking into his arm near the left wrist. A young man of Indian descent kneeled at his side and had his lips pressed against Harold's sleeve and the flesh beneath it. The teen snarled silently and ground his teeth into Hal's arm. Saliva stained the fabric. Pain flared and Hal caught a breath in his chest. He ripped his sleeve free of the teenager's mouth, taking a few teeth in the process and he slammed the stock of his rifle into the bridge of the man's nose. The blow tipped him backwards and sent him away. A return swing of his arm sent the barrel of his weapon into the eye socket of woman who wore a dress that probably cost a month of his military salary.

She went down in a bloody heap and just like that he had space to move.

Hal somehow used one leg and an arm to roll backwards from flat, performing the world's least attractive somersault in the midst of several undead attempting to murder him. He pushed up to a kneeling position and moving from left to right he snapped off three rounds into the hungry faces of the people who'd just tried to kill him. Surrounding them were a pile dead bodies dropped by Kevin.

Hal stood and looked at his arm, pulling up the sleeve. His brown skin had the half-moon impressions of teeth dug in but no blood. His sleeve and quick thinking had saved his arm and subsequently, his life. He laughed at Kevin and the contractor shot again. Hal's Marine unit moved on, the near death experience already being chalked up as something to drink heavily over later.

As the group made their way down the hill towards the street where the chopper above could land and spirit them away they fired every few seconds. The crash of gunfire deafened but it gave them what they needed to survive; space. Men would fire their guns until the bolts locked back and with deft, practiced hands they would remove their spent magazine and slap a new one home. The lull caused by their brief moment of reloading couldn't be perceived by sound alone. So many weapons kept firing there wasn't any sense of quiet.

Ten yards turned into twenty, and with each killed zombie —its head blown apart by a 5.56mm round—they came closer to an exit from the city and the million undead in it that had appeared out of nowhere.

"Guys, we need to move faster, we're not gonna make it shooting this much. We've got to run," Kevin the contractor said. He had his rifle moved to the side and had switched to his Glock handgun. He snapped off a few carefully aimed rounds and went to the side of the senator and the hobbling woman. She had kept herself together admirably despite every reason not to. Kevin hoisted her up with his left arm and tossed her over his shoulder in a carry reminiscent of a fireman exiting a burning building.

Hal was only a few feet away and he gave hand signals to his teammates to pick up the pace. A quick feel of his magazine pouches told him the contractor's assertion to move faster was spot-on. He'd already pissed through five of his eight magazines and at the rate they were still firing, they'd be out before they hit the end of the street and the chopper that hoped to land there.

As they moved, Hal heard Kevin call to the helicopter above for assistance.

"Fitz you gotta clear the way for us, we're almost dry on ammo down here," the man said using the microphones attached to his throat.

Hal walked at the tip of the group as they moved further downhill towards the Strand. The few cars still in the center of the city buzzed by, speeding without regard for any life save their own. He heard gunfire erupt from the sky above as his fellow unit members and the few contractors in the helicopter began to rain fire down on the undead they approached. Their inaccurate fire took longer to have an impact on the dead, but with the burden of killing spread the ground team's ammunition for the closest threats was protected. Hal dealt with the hungry attackers approaching with extreme prejudice.

As the men firing above grew accustomed to firing from the moving helicopter their shots became more accurate. Instead of four or five shots to a dead body it became three, then two and sometimes one. The rain of bullets toppled and crushed the wall of undead moving up the hill towards them with such rapidity the bodies were stacking up, and would soon become too high to walk over.

They ran.

One Marine without ammunition used his rifle like a battleaxe, smashing the stock into anything that got close to him. He sent one middle aged man wearing a David Bowie t-shirt straight through the heavy glass of a storefront. He might not be dead, but he wouldn't be stopping them from boarding the helicopter. Hal wondered if Bowie would be able to get on his spaceship in time to escape this mess and go home.

When they reached the end of the side street the chopper zoomed ahead and lowered itself between the brick buildings that framed the sidewalks. The cars passing had evaporated and somehow the Marines and the contractors had cleared out enough space that they could run to the helicopter and board before the undead could reach them. Their journey had come to an end.

As Hal approached the helicopter door opened and his fellow countrymen exited. They formed a perimeter around the helicopter and ushered the Americans into their transport. It seemed like the moment they took up firing positions the undead multiplied. Their gunfire grew and grew in volume until they drowned out the already loud rotors of the Lynx. The situation worsened by the second.

"Oi! Take me!" A bloodied and angry man screamed from the distance. One of Hal's friends—Danny, it looked like—took aim on the man and shot out his thigh with his rifle. The man went down as if he'd been walloped with a sledge at the knee. He cried out in pain and clutched at his ruined leg, framing the trench in his leg with his fingers and swearing a litany of curses. The undead on his heels collapsed on top of him, buying the Marines and their charges a few extra seconds from the danger in that direction.

The closest Marine to Hal tossed him a fresh magazine. He caught it in his offhand and slipped it into the first empty magazine pouch on his vest. He watched as Kevin placed the woman inside the helicopter and helped the senator aboard.

Hal caught the eye of Sergeant Beck. Beck had been aboard the helicopter that stayed aloft, and he'd been one of the guns providing fire support. Right now he stood from his shooting position and gave several of the Marines quick hand signals. He walked up to Hal as the Americans piled into the Lynx's rear passenger compartment. Beck grabbed Hal's vest at the shoulder and dragged him towards the helicopter. Right outside the door he yanked Hal closer, and spoke in his ear.

"Hal, you go with the Yanks. Keep the package safe. We'll

catch up. You try and get to your mum. Fuck the leave," Beck said.

"Wilco sir, thank you," Hal said with a nod, and leapt into the back of the helicopter.

Sergeant Beck tripped the transmitter switch on his microphone. "Go ahead on, boys. We'll make our way back to Buckingham Palace and reinforce them. You're heavy enough. God's speed."

"Roger that. Good luck, Beck," the pilot returned. A moment later the helicopter's engines roared, sending the downdraft out in a wash of trash and dirt. A few seconds later the wheels of the helo left the London street and the weight of the Lynx lifted carefully into the air. The liftoff was a storm of power under the control of the pilot. Beck didn't watch as it departed above and beyond for the Mildenhall air base.

"Boys, our job is done here. Let's move west to the palace. They could use us. And if they can't, we can certainly use that gate."

- Part Two -

For Queen and Country, but Mostly the Guy Next to Me

Sergeant Beck had his hands full. He'd sent his best man with the yanks on the Lynx to accompany them to the airbase they were supposed to go to. The decision cost him a shooter, but he knew Hal would make good decisions, and lead them to their next stop at Mildenhall. He hoped that sending the man away wouldn't cost the rest of the unit their lives as they made their way to Buckingham Palace.

Beck ran west down the center of the wide street, his rifle at the ready with the five men he needed to lead to safety at his back. He heard the loud snaps of sporadic weapons fire in the city as they ran. His own men shot at threats that had to be dealt with, adding to the mess. Those they could run past, they did. Ammunition was in too short a supply to shoot all the dead that London presented them with.

"Charlie Charlie, this is Echo Bravo One. Radio check, over," Beck said, sparing breath to speak as he ran.

Several seconds later he received a response. "Echo Bravo One this is Tango Charlie Forty. I read you three by four, over."

Three by four told Beck their radio signal wasn't the

strongest. He looked at the tall brick buildings and the steel and concrete towers of the city and cursed at them. They ate up the power and clarity of his communications.

"We are Oscar Mike to the palace. Package is enroute on one helo, one Marine as escort. Other vehicle is disabled at Covent Garden Market. We have multiple KIAs. Bodies in place. ETA thirty minutes. Over."

Beck heard the radio operator stammer. "Roger Echo Bravo One. We have no air assets to retask to support you. Can you supply a sitrep on the city conditions? Over."

Beck talked as he ran and his men fired their weapons. "Chaos, Tango Charlie Forty. Car wrecks, looting, citizen to citizen violence. We've engaged hundreds of violent people. It has for no discernible reason thinned out since the helo with the package left. Some of the people we've had to shoot do appear to be surviving lethal gunshot wounds. I hate to say this, but shots to the head are doing the trick. Over."

"Roger. Say again last? Over."

"Some of the people we are shooting are not dying. That or they are dying and continuing to attack us. Head shots appear to be lethal. Over." Beck laughed. The absurdity was profound.

"God's speed Echo Bravo One, For Queen and Country. Over."

"Roger. Out."

"So we're proper fucked, yeah?" Corporal Averill yelled during a lull in the fire. He hollered over the distant sirens that could be heard from the direction of rising plumes of smoke.

"Proper, yes," Beck replied, shouldering his rifle to fire, but holding his trigger finger straight. The man he'd seen stumble around the corner of an alley wasn't one of those… things, and he wasn't turning towards them. He got a reprieve, so long as he kept heading away from Beck and his team.

"What's the plan, Sarge?" the goofy and long faced private Motterhead asked. The slowest of the bunch, he had to yell loudly for Beck to hear him.

"Head to the palace and get inside their defenses is the goal. First step we procure ourselves ground transportation. Check the cars as we pass them, gents. Anyone know how to hotwire a car?"

No one responded.

"Well I suppose we should hope for keys. Everyone affix your night vision to your helmets and make a quick check of your ammunition."

The men rummaged on their chests and felt their full magazines. They barked out in sequence what their count was. "Three mags."

"Four mags."

"Four."

"Five," lance corporal Patil said.

"Three mags, sergeant."

"Patil, what are you waiting for? Five magazines. Shoot something please. Give a magazine to Thurgood so we all have four. Shoot anyone that approaches us with hostility. Motterhead and Thurgood move to the front. You're on car duty. Find us something we can start. Everyone else, cover them. We move west."

The men barked out their acknowledgment, and then moved. Not until after Patil gave his extra magazine to Thurgood and shot a shirtless man with a hole in his chest covered in a stranger's blood.

*****

"Bugger!" Motterhead belched as he ripped his hands away from a Volkswagon's door handle. "No keys."

On the other side of the street the smaller Thurgood echoed the statement. Beck spat on the ground and watched in the distance between the rows of brick and stone buildings as thousands of Londoners ran in the streets. Most had the good sense to run in the opposite direction of him and his unit.

"Move into the roundabout. Take up positions in the center," Beck shouted. His men moved.

They ran across the dead streets of the main thoroughfare with haste, threatening anyone who dared cross near them.

Scores of frightened residents and tourists who had hoped earlier for a photo with the lions of Trafalgar Square ran in every direction, all desperate to leave the overpopulated city and the danger posed by their fellow humans. In the distance Beck watched as a cop punted someone's very expensive digital camera on the ground as he too, ran away as fast as he could go. The camera hit the side of a building and exploded into a thousand shards of plastic.

"Fucking coward," Corporal Averill cursed as they formed a loose circle at the center of the roundabout near the famous lion sculptures. The Marines watched as the black uniformed policeman disappeared around a corner, heading north and away.

"I hope he gets bitten by one of those freaks. Do you think it's a bite that spreads it? Like in the movies?" Motterhead asked as he took a swig of water from his black plastic canteen.

"Shut up Motterhead," Corporal Averill said as he took a drink from his own bottle. "This isn't a movie."

"What if it's a book? What if we're characters in some asshole's shitty novel? What if he's written us as the victims that are intended to die? Which one of us do you think is the hero?" Motterhead asked. "I hope I'm the hero."

"Don't be daft, I'm the fucking hero," Beck said. "You're too ugly to be the hero. I'm Christopher Robin and you're our Eeyore. Now shut your bloody trap and cover your sector. Catch a breath."

A shot rang out behind Beck. The giant swarm of the crowds yelled and screamed louder, somehow picking up their pace. The violence of a gunshot in a normally peaceful place had to be horrifying. He turned and looked. A woman in her mid 20s was face down in the street, her pale arms and legs splayed wide. Her white purse was still clutched in her dying hand.

"She was approaching us, sir," Patil said. His Indian accent was still strong.

"You don't need to justify anything," Beck said, fishing out his own water bottle in the dying light of the day. "Just make sure she's down for good."

"Right," Patil said. He took aim, and blew a hole in the crown of her skull, sending bits of bone and flesh with the hair attached in every direction. Her leg twitched. Patil did too.

"How much further? It'll be dark soon," Averill said, adjusting his night vision goggles on their helmet mount. They didn't need the devices yet, but they might soon.

"We're a third. Maybe half. The mall will be good. Open territory to run," Beck said as he searched his brain for the map of the city. He tried to recall what they saw as they flew above not long before.

"That's at least another thirty minutes at the pace we're keeping," Averill said, angry.

"Aye," Beck said. "We need a car." But none had driven by since they started their run on the Strand. All the cars had somehow avoided coming in their direction. Perhaps it was their rifles, and the way they pointed them at everything that came their way.

"New plan," Beck said. "Guns down. We're scaring people away. We need someone to drive by us so we can appropriate a ride."

"Nick it?" Motterhead asked, lowering his rifle slightly.

"Borrow it. Perhaps just hop aboard for a few minutes."

From the direction of the north east up Charing Cross Road the boys heard the familiar noise of rubber wheels leaving skids on the pavement. Many of those fleeing from where they were headed in that direction and as the warriors watched, the crowd parted for a maniac vehicle coming directly towards them, speeding in the wrong direction on the city street.

"Guns at the ready," Beck said, taking a knee behind a light post and aiming his weapon at the oncoming and still unseen vehicle. As they prepared for the charge—their proverbial spears at the ready—the people of London scattered.

A black cab appeared. Its rounded, glossy form dashed through the crowd with remarkable deftness, avoiding the scared and uncoordinated with agility, squealing its tires at a constant rate to put space between it and the pedestrians.

Several desperate idiots reached out to try and open the doors of the cab only to have their knuckles broken and their fingers bashed. One man wearing an impeccable suit had his foot run over when he leapt at the vehicle's door handles. He dropped to the ground, clutching at his crushed foot, yelping in shock and pain.

At the wheel sat an old cabbie, his white hair wild and held in check by a dingy and stained flatcap. His eyes were wide but focused, and in the fray of his escape from or to something, his crazy eyes caught Sergeant Beck's, and the cab's brakes went into action, stopping the black taxi with a screeching sideways slide that vibrated the driver in his seat. The vehicle and its driver came to a stop two yards from the light post where Beck took cover. The gray haired driver turned his head and looked out the open cab window at Sergeant Beck, and tilted his head in the manner of a question.

"Buckingham Palace?" Beck said, extending his left arm slowly in the universal gesture to hail a cab.

The cabbie nodded as the throngs of people looked on, their mad exodus paused to watch the strange occurrence happening in the middle of one of London's most busy intersections. Beck's subordinate marines turned and watched.

"Forty Commando?" the cabbie asked the sergeant.

"Yes. Out of Taunton. We lost a chopper back at Covent Garden and are on foot to reinforce the Palace."

The cabbie hit a switch inside the taxi, and the white light of the TAXI sign turned on.

"Get in, but this ride'll cost the crown."

Beck hollered to his men, and somehow the five marines squeezed into the back of the London cab. As they peeled out heading west towards the Mall and the Palace, Beck watched as a trio of looters smashed the windows of businesses, and helped themselves to the goods they found.

He thought of the cop that ran away so fast.

*****

Smelly human sardines packed in a can, the cab peeled out and headed west, righting itself on the left side of the road as was proper. No feet were damaged in the return to full speed.

"Now in my day, when chaos reigned as it seems to today, we headed to the country. Cotswalds, as it were, or to the ocean to the north. Bombs rarely fell there. Someplace much safer than this city," the cabbie said, adjusting his hat.

Beck sat on the fold down jump seat to the man's left and peered out of the steering wheel. He watched as the taxi's meter ticked up and up, counting the price of their journey to the home of the British Crown.

"And furthermore, I don't see the need for this level of shite. What's the real deal with people today? A few car crashes, that helicopter of yours going down at the market, some little pricks buggering about stabbing folks. The cops'll have this in order soon enough," the old man rambled.

"I'm not sure about that," Beck said, attentive to the city passing by. The vehicle had passed under the Admiralty Arches a moment prior, and now sped along the Mall. Immediately the space opened up, with a wide road flanked by a wide sidewalk. Steel crowd control piping lined the street on both sides to help the visitors to London avoid walking into traffic. Three story tall government buildings already emptied of their workers sat on each side of the road behind the cover of the leaves of green trees under the darkness of the setting sun. Dusk was upon them, and the city's lights had yet to awaken. A dimness had taken over, and in its shadows demons hid.

"Oh?" the cabbie responded, his curiosity piqued. "Know something I should?"

"You *should* go to the country. Leave as soon as you drop us off at the Palace. Get your wife and whoever you care for and go. It isn't safe here right now. Might not be for a long time," Beck said as they passed a staggering man trying to maul all the passersby on the sidewalk. He had thick streams of dark red blood on his white dress shirt, marking where he'd caught at least one person already.

"Are they rabid?" the cabbie asked in a serious way. He

maneuvered the taxi right and left, crossing over the center line doing fifty miles an hour, dodging a pack of fleeing tourists and a car that had pulled over to render aid to someone on their back on the sidewalk. Beck saw the hurt man clutching at his torso. Beneath his fingers a large red stain spread.

"Something like that. We've only just been exposed to the situation. I can tell you this; once they go mad, they're a bitch to put down. Adrenaline keeping them up for far too long. The only way to put them down is to pop 'em in the head."

"Right in the fucking brain box," corporal Averill said. He sat in the rear-facing jump seat right behind the driver.

"Speaking of which, Sergeant, the fare for this joyride…" the cabbie said, eluding a woman carrying a toddler who didn't look the right way when she tried to cross the street. "Well I don't need any money."

Beck gave the driver a sideways glance. "What do you need?"

"I would appreciate it if your Browning and the spare magazines for it were to fall out on the floor of my taxi, Sergeant," the cabbie said flatly. He swerved once more and picked up speed as they hit a clear stretch of the dark street.

"I uh, I don't think that's a good idea," Beck said.

"I was at the Fall's curfew in Northern Ireland son. I know how to fire a weapon," the cabbie said, steering them around another threat to their progress. Up ahead Beck could see the barest hint of the roundabout in front of the palace. He could see some of the white stone building up from the crowd and the twinkle of the light bouncing off the gold statue at its top. He caught the vague image of an angel's wings and couldn't decipher whether it came from memory, or his actual sight. Cars and pedestrians fleeing in their direction obscured much of the ground `view.

"What side were you on?" Motterhead asked, a hint of challenge in his voice.

"Fuck you, son. I was first battalion, 52nd Lowland Volunteers. You shut your horse face pie hole or you can bloody well walk to the palace," the cabbie snapped off.

The rest of the men laughed.

"Give me your name and when this simmers down, I'll get it back to you. You've my word," the driver said.

"I'll see if the strap comes undone when we get out," Beck said. "That's the best I'll do for you."

"Well enough," the cabbie said. "Lock and load, boys. There's a bit of a crowd ahead. If you can get in touch with the men at the gate I'd advise it, Sergeant."

The windshield at the corner just above the driver's head cracked. A rifle or pistol round from ahead had impacted the glass, starring it with a round impression the size of a grapefruit. At the center of the impact the bullet remained, like a sliver lodged in the car's eye. The marines jerked away as the round snapped the glass. The cabbie stayed firm, unflinching.

The black cab's speed slowed as they came within a hundred yards of the traffic circle and the looming monument to Queen Victoria. Beyond the creamy stone front of Buckingham Palace rose like the castle it was. Atop the structure a gleaming white light shone upwards on the Union Jack, the flag of Britain.

"She's not home," Motterhead said, relieved.

"Judging by how they're shooting at the people nearby, you'd never know," Patil said in his quiet voice in the far back of the cab. That elicited a laugh from the rest of the men.

"Be ready," the cabbie said as he slowed the vehicle more. Several cars flew around the far border of the traffic circle at high speeds and sped past them, heading east. The escaping cars disregarded the safety of anyone nearby, clipping several bystanders who were trying to find their own safety. The cries of a young man clipped by a car's bumper and sent flying off his bicycle could be heard as they drove by.

The crowd seemed to be divided by their current occupation. The first group were the spectators unaware that they were in actual danger by standing or sitting where they were. Many of them were gathered on the monument at the center of the roundabout, taking pictures of the madness. The second group of people was the runners, the sweating, panting, frightened herd that had to get away as fast as they could manage. They ran over and past anyone who came between them and where they thought they were going, making the situation worse for everyone else. The third and final group was those laying active siege to the castle gates.

They ran and leapt over the rows of crowd fencing and charged at the sturdy fortifications that protected the Queen and her home. The reached for the black bars that separated the masses from the crown, and they threw everything they could in the faces of the guards charged with protecting the Queen's home. They screamed for justice, for safety, for answers, for mercy. They didn't get far, and few received mercy.

The policemen who stood inside the thick enameled bars of the Palace walls carried MP5 submachineguns, and after barking out a hundred or more warnings as they dodged cans, bottles, rocks and all manner of projectiles, the men wearing the black body armor and black riot helmets shot carefully at the people trying to climb the metal fortification. They started with intentional wounding shots to the legs, but when the crowd trying to gain entrance to the palace started to throw debris they ramped up the deadliness of their response. Their carefully aimed rounds moved from legs to hips, hips to stomachs, and as the attackers became more enraged the rapidity of the police's shots increased, and their accuracy dropped. Errant rounds flew into the city's distance, striking unknown victims.

When the black cab carrying the marines came to a stop on the opposite side of the Queen Victoria memorial it wasn't because they couldn't drive around it. The cabbie stopped them because if they drove past the stone they would have no cover from the steadily increasing rate of gunfire.

"Best let 'em know you're here," the taxi driver said. "And kindly if you would, I think this is your stop."

The back doors of the cab popped open without Beck's orders. The men knew they were sitting ducks in the stopped car and as they exited they had their guns up, protecting the vehicle and their fellows. Last of them all, Beck opened his door as he watched over the steps of the monument as the gunfire died off.

"Thank you. Stay safe," he said, then shut the door.

"Oi! About that-" the cabbie yelled at the closing door. On the floor of the cab below the jump seat rested Beck's Browning 9mm, and two spare magazines.

Turns out the snap on the holster was loose after all.

The cabbie floored the gas pedal in his little black taxi, and sped off towards west London, and a very uncertain future.

- Part Three -

The Last Few Steps

The men were crouched behind the monument in the dark of the first full hour of evening. They had been pinned down trying to radio the palace for almost an hour. Streetlights lit the world around them, and cast shadows in all directions. Beyond the close orange orbs of the streetlights distant fires lit the night. One exceptionally large fire to the west lit the horizon beyond the roof of the palace. The flames had erupted, casting their orange light against the roof of the clouds after a massive explosion not long ago. A crashed airplane perhaps, or a fuel truck.

Gunfire popping off in bursts from the palace was sporadic, but steady, and the crowds watching were the same. They had flocked to the sides of the streets and found cover but they still watched and filmed, lured in by the glory of violence and wanting to be near a calamitous event in history. Beck was certain they were idiots.

"Any luck?" Beck asked Patil.

"Naught," Patil said. "I can't get them at all. Forty Commando is trying to get in touch with the Palace for us but they aren't responding. They are saying Heathrow is eating up resources left and right. I guess a plane crashed. Ran out of fuel."

He could hear the planes circling miles above when the gunfire paused. "What the hell does that have to do with us?" Beck asked. "How did communications get so shit, so fast?"

"Can you imagine how crushed the phone service is? Look around. There has to be five hundred 999 calls running right now, and then for every phone ring there's a radio dispatch to an emergency service. Then there's the pricks on their cell phones calling for mum and dad," Patil said, giving up trying to contact anyone. "Ten million pricks all screaming at the same time."

"That's a lot of pricks," Thurgood muttered.

"Shut up," Beck said. "Alright, brilliant. If we approach, we stand a good chance at getting shot. If we leave this cover, we stand a good chance at getting shot. If we remain here, we stand a good chance at being bitten or beaten to death. So, let's let them know we're here, identify ourselves the old fashioned way, and move to flank. Motterhead, get ready to throw smoke. Everyone else, get ready to move." Beck got out a smoke grenade.

The horse-faced giant nodded and yanked a tubular smoke grenade from a pouch on his belt. He moved his rifle to the side and pulled the pin in unison with his sergeant.

Beck hurled his grenade with all the strength he could muster into the courtyard separating the monument from the gate. The same courtyard that saw tens of thousands of tourists every month, but had now been turned into the scene of a massacre. Motterhead saw where it landed, and threw his short of the spot.

The two grenades popped loudly and issued out massive streams of dense white smoke. The devices hissed and spat as the thick cloud shot across the ground and into the still June air, forming a wall of smoke.

"ROYAL MARINES! FORTY COMMANDO APPROACHING! HOLD YOUR FIRE!" Beck screamed. "Follow me. Head to the left gate. Do not return fire if they shoot." Beck took off trotting in a crouch, using the monument's circular retaining wall as cover. When he ran out of that real estate, he jogged along the line of the spreading smoke, taking care to give the bodies of the wounded attackers a wide berth. Beck's men followed him, spacing themselves out to avoid bunching up.

"TO THE LEFT GATE, MARINES!" a voice yelled out.

"ROGER THAT!" Beck hollered back to the stranger.

A gentle breeze picked up, and the wall of smoke slid over the top of the line of runners. In the time it took to take a breath, they had been swallowed up by the viscous cloud. Their visibility had evaporated and Beck slowed to a trot, then a walk. The dense smoke killed the noise of the battlefield, and sent them back two hundred years into the past.

"Go to night vision?" Private Thurgood asked in the orange-lit cloud of smoke.

"It won't help," Corporal Averill replied. "We need thermal to see through the smoke. Bugger this shit."

"Watch out for the fucking bodies. No one trip!" Beck snapped. He knew they were walking through the edge of where the wounded and dead lay. He could hear the moans of the injured and dying in the haze.

"Soldier, please help. They shot me. Help me please I'm bleeding badly," a man called out. Beck couldn't even see where he was, but he was close.

"Fuck off, prick," Motterhead said to him. "Got what you had coming to ya, ya did."

"Please. I'm begging you," the voice said again. "Oh thank you, if you could just take my hand—aaahhh!" the man started screaming. The marines backed away from the sound of the voice, trying to put space between the man and whatever was making him scream bloody murder.

"Move boys. Quick," Beck said. The injured man screamed again. Someone else in the impenetrable smoke screamed too. Out of fear or pain, they couldn't tell.

"What the fuck is happening out there?" Motterhead exclaimed as the unit picked up speed, shuffling their feet in the impenetrable dark.

"Run boys!" the same policeman's voice hollered from somewhere inside the palace's gate. "They're starting to get up and head your way!"

"Shit," Beck said to himself. He prayed for clear space, and bolted. The sounds of his men's feet on the courtyard stone told him they did too. His legs pumped up and down, putting one boot in front of the other with a slap as he ran. Each stride his mind braced for a trip, either a piece of curb or a dead body. He prayed for smooth stone, he prayed to stay upright.

He tripped.

Something caught his right ankle and he lost his balance. Time dilated as he launched forward into white space, feet above the hard stone above. Beck tried to tuck, to roll onto his back so he'd land on his shoulder on the stone but something had his foot in a grip. It almost felt like he'd been snared by a trap his boot felt so tight. His forward momentum halted, he plummeted to the hard ground below.

Something cracked in his shoulder, or maybe his chest. Stars flew in front of his eyes and his breath shot out of his mouth in a gust. He gasped and tried to remain as still as he could to halt the pain in his shoulder. He reached down to his hip to grab the pistol there as he felt hungry, clawing hands and a heavy weight move up his leg.

His hand found an empty holster at the moment he felt a sharp, piercing sensation just above his kneepad.

"Mother fucker!" he yelled as his men reached and passed him. They stopped when they heard his scream. Beck began punching down at the burning sensation in his leg. His right fist connected with someone's face, and he followed the blow with another from his left fist. One after another he grunted in exertion and pain as he pummeled the person biting his leg.

"Hold still," he heard lance corporal Patil say in a panic. Looming above him he saw the form of the marine lean over, rifle aimed flat to the earth at the body of the person attacking him. Patil fired a single shot into the side of the head of the person biting Beck, and the pain in Beck's leg ceased. He dug his fingers into the mouth of the asshole who hurt him and dug the jaw open, scraping his finger and a nail on the sharp edge of a broken tooth. The teeth came free with a shock of pain, a run of his own hot blood, and he backed away on the ground. The body of his attacker fell off his lower leg, all dead weight. Two of his men scooped him up and with another grunt of pain, they helped him hobble off through the fog of war.

The pain in his leg was extraordinary, but he stayed upright with the help of his men.

As they exited the cloud of smoke they saw one of the black and gold gates crack open ahead. Five heavily armed policemen stood behind the protective steel, their weapons trained on them, and the threat of whatever still stalked in the smoke. The marines slipped through the gap in the gate and over the lifted anti-car blockade. Lifting his leg cost Beck notable pain, but they were safe. He'd delivered his men.

"Christ you need a medic," an elderly cop with a MP5 and a mustache almost as dangerous said. "Is that gunshot? Or a bad bite there?"

"Is there a doctor or medic inside?" Beck asked with a wince.

"Aye," he said. "We're glad to have you. This day has been hell and is heading to worse. We'll be the richer to have you and your boys here, Sergeant."

"Thank you," Beck said. He turned to Motterhead, Hodges and Averill. "You three cover the gate with these men and women. Patil and Thurgood, would you help a chap to the infirmary? Constable could you spare us a guide. Marines don't know the way here. We aren't always invited to Royal affairs."

"Of course. We'll get you patched up right quick. Follow me," the mustache said.

As they walked away—the two marines helping the third—Beck felt something like relief. Maybe it was shock setting in, but it felt good to him. He'd gotten all of the men who had survived the helicopter crash to the palace, safe and sound. He would forever regret the loss of his medic, Corporal Adamson, but he clung to the idea he'd done right by the rest.

"Good job, lads. You're good men."

Patil adjusted the weight of his sergeant. "Thank you sir. You'll be back at it in no time."

Patil was right. He'd survive a little bite, and then he'd track down that cabbie and get his pistol back.

It'd be brilliant.

—An Elmoryn Short Story—

Roots Grown Deep

"Sure is hot this summer," Lily Thornbrooke muttered. "It's near high moons above and far from dawn and I'm sweating like a lamb in an oven."

Lily's cousin Raymond Thornbrooke—a willowy tall boy still aching through his last puberty growth spurt—sat beside her on a wooden bench atop one of the two gatehouses that greeted travelers to their small village of Low Marish. The red moon Hestia above was near to full and bright red like a child's cherry flavored sucker. Following the red moon across the black night was the blue-white orb of Lune, Elmoryn's other moon.

"Aye, you're not wrong. This leather armor has chapped everything on my body it's touched since I put it on after dinner. I can't wait for dawn to get it off," Ray said as he adjusted the rest of his toughened leather breast. He picked up his bow from the wooden crenellations he and Lily guarded their town behind and tried to puff out his chest. The two may be related, but that was no reason to not look manly in her presence.

"We've a couple hours to go," Lily said, brushing back a sweaty strand of her dark brown hair. She tucked it behind her ear where hopefully it'd stay for ten minutes.

"Aye. You have any water left?" Ray asked her. "All this staring into the woods, waiting to see one of our dead neighbors walking towards the wall has me thirsty."

"Yeah, here," she said and handed him a clay jug filled with fresh river water. He removed the rubber stopper and took a swig.

"Still cool. Thank you," Ray said. "When do you suppose this will all end?"

"I wish I knew. Father Burke says these people from the woods are not undead. His spells have been almost no use to stop them," Lily said, leaning over the edge of the raised wall to peer into the depths of the southern forest. A drop of sweat ran off her chin and spattered on a wide leaf far below. She lifted her head and looked up over the forest, over the horizon she couldn't see towards the nation she'd never visited. Ebonvale was to the south. A land of strange people with a strange language that only they spoke. Brave people, but unwelcoming people. Not too unlike the people of her own nation; The Shires.

"He's daft. Gotten into his ceremonial wine one too many times. You saw the man yesterday, didn't you? He walked like the dead, staggering all about. Distant eyes, saliva everywhere. Going angrily at the first person he saw. A blind man could see he was the undead."

"I think Father Burke is right," Lily said.

"How?" Ray laughed. "And how would a girl know what was undead and what wasn't?"

"How would you? Tell me how many times you've laid eyes on the walking dead? How many people on your side of the family didn't make it to an apostle to be blessed before coming back to kill? Hm?" She already knew the answer. No one in their family had succumbed to the curse of Elmoryn.

"Well… I… It's just…"

She leaned over the thick wooden logs that made up Low Marish's wall and tried to ignore his rambling attempt at saving face. A crack of a stick breaking alerted her to movement below.

"Are you listening to me?" Ray asked, frustrated.

"Quiet," she whispered, holding a finger to her lips. She then pointed the dirt smudged digit over the top of the wall until it pointed in the general direction of where she heard the noise. Ray pulled a long wooden arrow from a quiver that hung on his belt and notched its feathered shaft on his bow's string. Lily did the same and the two family members peered again into the black of the woods below.

Another branch broke.

Ray looked around and jogged down the wall to a wrought iron sconce. He lifted the torch out of the cone shaped iron placement and came back, holding its light and smoke aloft. He left a trail that looked like a rising steam engine's stack as he went.

"Watch out," he said and threw the torch off the wall.

The flaming stick tumbled end over end as it fell, casting off a wild spiral of smoke, embers and sparks. The leaves of the tall trees cast insane shadows as the orange and yellow light from the fire spun again and again. The torch bounced off a thick clump of branches and leaves, the hit the damp forest floor with a faint thud. The flame almost died out from the fall and impact, but after a few moments of sizzling away the moisture surrounding it, the torch flared back to life, illuminating the underbrush and forest floor.

A figure walked past the flame.

"Sweet shit," Lily exclaimed, grabbing Ray's arm tightly.

"Ow, damn Lily. That hurt," Ray said, swatting her grip from his bicep. He'd bruise the next day, he was sure of it.

"Shush, watch it. Pay attention," she said, already having moved past their earlier argument.

Down below the person walked with an uncoordinated limp past the fallen torch. One leg seemed to be lame; causing a limp or stagger that a healthy man would've tried harder to hide, or fix. Both arms hung strangely limp at the waist, failing to move with the motion of the legs, sending the walker further off-balance. A protruding root tripped up the stranger's good foot, causing a forward fall that resulted in the intruder falling straight to the ground against a rock, winding up in a thorny bush. They didn't cry out in pain, or even gasp. After a few seconds, the now bloody interloper gathered themselves and got to their feet.

"See? Dead as lamb's wool," Ray said.

"No, he's not dead at all. He's bleeding. Dead men don't bleed," Lily said.

Ray turned his attention down to the blood-soaked person pulling themselves up using a tree trunk. Sure enough she was right. The filthy yellow shirt the emaciated man wore had a hundred pinpricks of red welling larger and larger. The thorns had spoiled the undead answer, but raised another.

What caused the living to act like the dead?

"What do we do?" Ray asked.

"Fetch the captain of the guard. He'll be walking the walls somewhere. I'll watch this fellow while you're gone. Be quick about it," Lily said.

Ray looked at her, then at the frightening apparition walking less than twenty feet below, then he took off running.

"Show me," Acton Cobb said to Lily. The captain of the guard had just arrived at the spot along the wall Lily and Ray had seen the wounded, staggering man wander. Acton had his own bow—one much larger and more powerful than the teen's—at the ready. A wide-headed arrow sat on the string, ready to cut the strange person down.

"Here," Lily said, pointing down at the base of the wall.

Acton's height made it easy for him to see downward. He leaned over through one of the archer notches of the wall and peered down. In the shadows he saw movement, but with the moons at his back he couldn't identify what was happening in the dark. He tugged on his brown beard and thought.

"Fetch another torch," he asked as two more village guards arrived, their bows at the ready. Ray scampered away and came back, holding another cloth-wrapped, pitch-soaked torch.

The flame burned bright as he handed it to the older, bearded leader of the town's defenses.

"Thank you, Acton said as he took it. He leaned back over and dropped it carefully lengthwise a few feet from the shuffling intruder below. It fell straight to the grass below, and cast light on the man scratching his nails off on the log wall below.

"By my mother's spirit, that's Grant Barber," Acton exclaimed. An expression of sickness washed over the captain's face as the man now known as Grant looked up at Acton with oddly discolored eyes. Grant didn't snarl like a hungry wolf, or reach up to attack like a normal undead would. Instead he looked about as if he were in a stupor and trying to figure out how best to reach the familiar face above.

"Grant Barber? Son of Hadwell and Celine Barber?" Lily asked, shocked. "Don't they live a few miles south of Low Marish? You think he walked all the way here at night? Like that?"

Acton leaned back inside the protective barrier of the wall. "He must've. Walking toward the torch lights on the wall I surmise. Grant took a wife from Leister a few months ago, at the end of spring. I knew him to be building a new farmhouse for his wife a mile from his parents. Carving it out of the woods. The deeper woods."

"That's never good," Ray said. "He might've... disturbed something in the trees. Something that did whatever to him."

"No," Acton said. "I think he might've disturbed *the tree*."

"There's a... *special tree* in the woods?" Lily asked, her voice trembling more than a little.

Acton looked her dead in the eye. "It's been dormant for longer than I've been alive. They thought..."

"What?" Ray asked.

"We thought it had died. They thought it did, at least. We have to gather the clan elders. They'll remember what happened last time. Keep this man from leaving the wall. Throw a fishing net over his head if you have to. I'll wake the elders. Dawn approaches."

The central clan hall of the village of Low Marish warmed up to intolerable levels by the dawn's break. The heat and humidity in The Shires had reached epic proportions earlier in the summer, making most homes and structures uncomfortable for the entire season. The vaulted-roofed log hall lit by torches and filled with the scared residents of Low Marish boiled up and over far worse and long before the sun's heat caressed the thatched roof. The meeting couldn't last, or they'd cook to death.

At the center of the rectangular room lay a triangular table. On each flat side rested a smooth wooden chair, each high-backed and carved with the surname of the Shire clan that held seat at the table of Low Marish.

The gentrified, stooped form of Opal Thornbrooke sat in the chair that bore her family's name. A thin mesh shirt hung on her frail shoulders, covering her pale flesh minimally. On her face she wore a scowl. Her knotted, arthritic fingers thrummed on the table as she assessed her clan peers.

A full decade younger and to her left sat Elder Cobb, Acton's grandfather and sitting master of the village's emaciated commerce. His bulbous red nose and patchwork flush gave away his love for ale and mead but his narrowed, shrewd eyes were focused. He too disapproved of being roused so early, but he arrived, as was his duty.

The final elder reached his seat with the help of two younger family members. The wizened body of Father Burke leaned against the armrest of the wooden seat as it were giving him the strength to breathe. His bony arms wobbled as he rested his long back against the suitably tall chair. His white robes cascaded around him like a loose bathrobe, covering only the most crucial of private areas. His pasty chest was exposed, as was the flaccid flesh of his long legs. Flanking him only a few feet away was his grandson, the next resident apostle in line when Father Burke passed on.

The residents of Low Marish hushed as the final elder cleared his throat.

"Glad to see your spirit is still inside your skin, Father," Opal said with a wry, wrinkled grin.

"Well Opal, it's fighting to get out each and every day. I yearn for the day I can cast aside this silly body and float around haunting you and your family like a proper friend ought. One day you'll get your wish, as will I. No need to rush what doesn't need rushing," Father Burke said back to her.

"Stop flirting," Elder Cobb chastised. "We've business to attend to. My boy brings news from the wall." Elder Cobb looked over his shoulder with great effort, and waved, summoning his son.

Acton approached, stepping up on the raised dais the triangular table sat atop.

"What say you, captain of the guard?" Opal asked of the tall, bearded warrior.

"We have identified a wandering man outside the wall. Young Lily and Ray Thornbrooke spotted him no longer than two hours past. I identified him as Grant Barber," Acton said.

"Son of Celine and Hadwell?" Opal asked, her memory sharp.

"True."

"Is he dead? Shall we send Priest Burke to banish him back to the earth? Such a shame for a soul to be lost," Elder Cobb said.

"No, he's not dead at all," the captain said. "Nor is he quite alive in the normal sense. I ordered him kept at the wall while we gathered. He appears… off." He looked down to his feet and the leather boots he wore.

"Say again? Am I so old as to have heard you say he's still alive, but wandering like the dead we've had of late?" Opal asked, holding her hand to her ear and making a cone shape.

"He is not dead, though he acts it. His eyes are faded and

glossy, streaked dark with... something. He staggers and stumbles, but he is not enraged as the dead are. He seeks no death, but he seeks something. Similar to the other man who was encountered and killed by the Glenshire tradesman on the road the other day. I think he might've succumbed to something else."

"Sick with discordant balance? Bone rot?" Father Burke suggested.

"No," Acton said. "I suspect it might be something older, something we have dealt with long before. I think the Barbers built too close to the ravager tree, and somehow roused it."

The three elders coughed and laughed at the incredulous statement. There was no way...

"The Barber's family farm is but a mile from where the old maps showed the tree. Grant Barber is just wed, and I know he broke ground to start a home for his own family. I believe he did so a mile from his mother and father's, which would put him perilous close to the tree. If he were to have accidentally roused a pod of spores..."

Opal stopped laughing first. Father Burke and Elder Cobb saw her face as she twisted through the halls of her memory and realized that she'd remembered something. Something important.

"Elder Opal? Do you have something to say? Something to tell me?" Acton asked, resting his hand on the pommel of his long sword.

"My mother told me the ravager tree only spawns during hot, long summers."

"I thought I had remembered it so," Acton said. "What else?"

"Once a hundred years, give or take the moon's cycle or two," Opal said. "It's been about that time since the last season, if memory serves."

"Impossible," Elder Cobb said. "The ravager tree is a legend. A story told to gardeners and farmers to keep them out of the furrows of their fields and in their beds at night. We're imagining ghosts where there are none."

"Father, it is worth my time to leave the village and investigate, is it not? If I am wrong then all we've given away is a walk in the woods. If Opal and I are right… then we could save everyone in Low Marish from a terrible death. Or what amounts to life with the ravager tree awake."

Elder Cobb scoffed at his son.

"Acton if what you believe is true, we could lose the whole village," Father Burke said. "If the mother tree can infect enough animals and people outside the walls, it'll surround us, and plant more of its kind until we cannot leave our own walls. Eventually it will plant us all in the ground to feed on. It's only a matter of time. Either we act swiftly, or we die slowly."

An angry young mother stood in the crowd. She clutched at two fat, happy babies on her hips.

"What are you talking about? Ravager tree? Spores? Speak truths to the people. To your families. Some of us have children we'd like to give futures to," the mother scolded.

"Sit, child. I watched you born and you'll watch your grandchildren born the same I did. Don't let the old apostle's doom saying spoil your milk," Opal said gently. "Though like all words cobbled together, there's a message in what is said."

"If it lies in the woods where the maps say it is, how do I kill it?" Acton asked as the woman with the two children sat.

"You don't kill it. Ravager trees can't be killed in the way people can," Opal said. "But you can put it back to rest for another century. Maybe we can figure out how to kill it with that time."

"Then tell me how to do that, and I'll see the task done," Action said.

Opal remembered that too.

"It is as Opal said," Acton mused. "Grant is infected by the ravager tree." Acton, Lily, Ray and Powell Burke, the third in command of the city guard stood over the netted form of Grant Barber. As he'd suggested in the early morning several hours prior they had thrown a fishing net over him, and he'd tangled his feet up and fallen. Acton crouched over the oddly calm form of Grant and looked closely into his eyes.

The whites were losing ground to faint green and black streaks that fed in from the sides. Roots of the ravager tree spores spread from inside the man's skull.

"What is that?" Lily asked.

"When a spore pod bursts, and the released cloud inhaled, the ravager tree infects a man. The cloud is a million tiny seeds that take root in your mouth, throat and brain. Somehow the tree can control those infected to do its bidding. Instead of waiting for rain the tree sends out its infected to gather sustenance for it."

"Sustenance?" Ray asked, voice shaking.

"People, animals. When the spores grow to a point where the brain and body cannot contain them any longer they return to the tree and die, giving their life blood to the roots of the tree," Acton said, then stood.

"The tree eats people?" Ray asked.

"It's a big tree. Infused with The Way I would venture. Something dark from our world's past. Something from before The Fall three centuries ago."

"I say we burn it," Powell said as he leaned on his spear, clinking the rings on his leather armor against the ash haft. Powell carried a massive pack on his back that clearly weighed a great amount. Even with his substantial size the bag seemed to bother him.

"Opal said the tree might not catch. Its bark is too tough. But there is something we can do. Fire has a home in this fight. We brought the flasks of lamp oil, right?"

Lily and Ray lifted satchels up from their hip. Faint clinking could be heard from the bag's interiors, like clay wind chimes on a distant neighbor's porch.

"Good then," the tall Powell said. "I say we move now, burn everything and come home for a late lunch to celebrate. This bag makes my back ache."

"Leave it to a Burke to plan the celebration before we attain victory," Lily said.

"Leave it to a Thornbrooke to not keep their mouth shut," Powell said, taking up his spear and pointing it at the younger girl. The pair grinned.

"Thomas, Mattias," Acton yelled as he looked up to the top of the city's wall where several guards stood by, watching. "Summon Priest Burke for a blessing of soul's rest, and give Grant Barber peace. This man has told us his story. We head south."

The four left the wall, and headed south towards the horror that waited.

Acton Cobb led a small party of Low Marish residents into the southern forest. Unlike his subordinate Powell Burke he'd listened to the advice of the Elder Opal and shorn his black leather armor for the trip. The crushing heat made the armor almost a danger to wear for that reason alone but Opal warned that the fight they faced wouldn't be decided by the thickness of hide any of them wore.

They would need speed and wits, not brute force and tough armor.

The four walked in the light of the rising sun along the south-eastern trade road for almost two miles. They kicked rocks and dirt on the cart-worn road and watched the surrounding fields of burnt wheat and grass pass. They drank profuse amounts of water from jugs and skins and when they crossed the arched stone bridge halfway to their goal, each refilled from the cold running stream below.

When the four passed over the crest of a small hill Acton stopped them. A farm lay nestled in the crux of a forest's elbow, surrounded by wooden fences and flanked by a long, flat barn. The bodies of sheep lay in the field, beaten to death.

"Look there, and there," Acton said as he pointed into the field. "Sheep killed, then dragged into the woods to the east. See the scuff marks in the rows?"

They all saw.

"Protect your faces," the captain said. He produced a dark wedge of cloth from his belt and poured out a handful of water into it. When sufficiently soaked he wrapped the fabric around his lower face, forming a mask to cover his nose and mouth. In the old books the ancestors of Low Marish said this would protect them from the spores.

Lily, Ray, and a very sweaty Powell did the same. Acton checked over their masks and when he was satisfied, they walked down the road and jumped the fence that marked the border of the Barber family farm. Following the trail the dragged sheep bodies left after that was easy work.

Ray's hand shook, wobbling the bow he held as if a winter wind blew fierce against it. He prayed for a winter wind. It would distract him from his guilt for being scared and cut the heat in the dark of the forest. No wind would come, however. Not in this long, hot summer.

From behind the tree he crouched at he looked to the left and right quickly, trying to forget what sat in front of him. To his right he saw the large Powell Burke as he slid the giant bag off of his back and undid the leather straps that held it shut. The man looked calm in the presence of danger, no different than a hunter stalking a deer. Cautious.

To his left Ray saw a very frightened Lily holding her bow

in equally shaky hands. His instinct to protect her grew suddenly, even though he knew she was the better shot, older, and more brave than he. He laughed at his folly and looked for Acton.

The visage of the tree interrupted his search.

The four explorers had found the ravager tree easily. Following the trail of scuff marks and blood smears had been a child's task. The minions of the tree had made no effort to conceal their works.

Each of the bodies dragged through the forest were brought to a circular clearing the ravager tree occupied the center of. Dominated the center of. The ancient tree looked as much like a monster as it did a plant. Five men holding hands would've struggled to encircle the base of its trunk and it reached to the sky a hundred feet above the large oaks, maples, and pines gathered fearfully around it. At its base were pomegranate sized red globes that tantalized like ripe, delicious fruit. They almost pulsated with visible danger from the spores that lay in wait inside them.

Spaced equally around the gargantuan trunk were branches that left the center mass at a steep angle, aimed at the sky. The branches reached their sharp zenith then twisted at an elbow and stabbed sharply down as if the tips were heavy, and couldn't finish the climb to the clouds. The branches ended in sharp spikes that slowly moved side to side, like a horrid wind blew even in the stillness of the cursed glade. Not a single leaf grew on the tree.

Littered around it were hunched human figures, their knees in the dirt and their hands digging at the soil. Ray watched one by one as they methodically scratched out grave after grave for the pile of bloody, dead animals they had dragged there who knows how long before. The mother Barber stood up on shaky legs and turned with great care. She grabbed a goat carcass and pulled it into the hole. When she was satisfied of the lay of it, she stepped away and began to dig another hole a few feet away.

Then, like a strike of lighting, one of the ravager tree's

dagger branches snapped down. It impaled the goat body into the hole and split its torso in half, spilling fresh entrails and rotten meat into the hole. The branch drew out of the corpse and into the air and then slammed down with a ground shaking impact, ruining the body further. Ray cried as he watched the animal's form lose its familiar shape and become bones and gore held together by strips of skin and hide.

Something moved underneath it in the hole. Black fingers, long ropy strands of cartilaginous fibers rose from the dirt and earth high enough to wrap themselves around the mess of the goat. The tree's roots embraced another meal. Ray watched as the flesh of the animal was pulled deep into the earth for the ravager to suckle upon.

On the far side of the carnage and the slow drones of the Barber family servicing the tree, Ray watched as Acton stalked elegantly. He moved low and alternated his foot speed to move from tree to bush, from boulder to draw. He evaded the root-filled eyes of the almost dead and the strange almost supernatural watch of the eyeless ravager tree.

In one hand he held his long sword, in the other an unlit torch. Ray lost himself in the motions of the brave and very alone captain as the man took a knee and sat down the rag-wrapped torch. Acton poured out a bottle of lamp oil on a large dry bush covered in emaciated blueberries and produced his flint and steel. Two strikes later he had the torch lit and two ticks after that the bush went up like a funeral pyre in Low Marish's central square.

The effect the flame had was instantaneous.

Hadwell and Celine Barber stood from their holes in the earth and began to stride angrily across the ground the ravager tree owned. Slower still was an unidentified woman who struggled to move at all. She twitched and stumbled, but moved towards Acton nonetheless. The spore-dominated servants of the tree came to their matron's aid.

That must be Grant's wife, Ray thought, feeling better somehow that the spore-infested people were moving away from him at last.

"Boy," Powell said in a whisper. "Boy!"

Ray turned to the massive guard. "Yes, sorry."

"I must sow the field with the twice blessed salt as Acton draws their attention. You two are to protect me with the bows. Do you understand?"

"What do we shoot? The tree?" Ray asked, confused.

"No, idiot. Shoot the people if they come for me. The tree is no danger if I stay far enough away from its branches and red bags of spores at its roots," Powell said, producing a handful of small burlap bags filled with salt from his backpack. He hefted them in one hand and grabbed the strap of the larger pack.

"I'm ready," Ray said. "Though I've never killed before."

"I am ready too," Lily said from further down the line. She didn't echo Ray's second statement. Ray wasn't sure what that meant.

Powell moved without hesitation. He dragged his backpack ten yards into the clearing and dropped it, allowing the smaller mismatched bags inside to spill out for easier access. One by one he tore open the bags in his hands with his teeth and emptied their contents out into the dug holes filed with gore and blood. One bag became three, three bags became six and then he was out. He ran back to the backpack and its resupply of the poisonous salt.

As he ran, the tree felt the burning sting of the salt, and it reacted.

Over and over the massive hooked branches with their spear-like tips stabbed into the ground near to where he ran. The massive impacts of the blade-like branches grew closer and closer to his feet as he tried desperately to pick up speed. The tree felt his girth come down on the ground, one foot at a time, and Ray watched as one branch held high, twitched once as it measured the time of it, then descended down.

The tree's limb came down and skewered poor Powell through the back and belly, knocking him off his feet and to the ground, impaling him still on the unsalted earth he tried to escape over.

"Gah," Powell gasped, spitting up a lungful blood. He

clawed at the earth, digging furrows into the grass and exposing the bones of others who had miss-guessed the reach of the ancient, evil tree. He looked from Ray's face to the arm bone of a child, then closed his eyes and let his head hit the ground.

"Powell!" Ray yelled.

"Shut your mouth!" Lily said through gritted teeth. "The tree will find us. Fire your bow at the men and women going after Acton. I'll spread the salt." She got to her feet and began to take off her quiver and satchel filled with oil.

"No," Ray said, faking bravery. "I'll do it. I'm faster and stronger."

"You're not faster than me. Don't be stupid. I'm lighter. It must feel where you walk. The tree won't find me as easily." Lily didn't wait for him to argue. She strode out of the trees and straight towards the large bag filled with apostle-blessed salt.

"Lily! What if you're wrong?" Ray blurted, trying to get her to turn back, but his cousin either didn't hear his whisper, or ignored him. He shook the sweat from his eyes and the fear from his paralyzed fingers and drew the string on his bow. He found the stumbling shape of Hadwell Barber and lined up a shot into the man's back. With unsure fingers he let the arrow fly.

It fell short of the man's shoulders, but still plunged into the flesh of his hamstring. The elder Barber fell to his knees, buying Acton time to set another bush aflame and put space between he and mother Barber.

As Ray lined up a second shot Lily lifted four of the small bags in her tiny hands. She tucked two into her trouser pockets and a third into her armpit. With her dagger she cut open the top of the last. She flung the bag's contents in a wide arc then tossed it aside. Another dagger slash later she tiptoed ten feet around the area of the tree and emptied the second bag. Above her head the branches of the ravager tree twitched and seized, reaching out like the arms and legs of a spider too large to wrap a sane mind around.

One of the branches dipped straight at her, almost daring her to move, or spread salt. She froze—more still than the trees that watched from feet away—and waited for the branch to forget her.

A thousand heartbeats and ten seconds later it did, and she moved once more.

"Keep at it!" Acton yelled as he emptied out another vial of oil in the brush. "Spread the salt as I set the fires. Good job, girl! The earth shall rot under it as the world burns around it!"

She smiled against the fear that threatened to empty her bladder and nodded at the man's commands. She emptied the third bag and moved slowly and emptied the fourth. Empty, she returned on the balls of her feet to the pile of bags.

Powell's hand launched out and tried to grab her foot.

A scream punched at the inside of her teeth but he kept her mouth shut. The dead man had returned to undeath fast and were it not for the branch that held him fast to the ground he'd have stood and killed her. His eyes had drained of color until they were whitened over with the rage of the undead. His face had twisted into a grimace of soul-trapped anger and pain, and he sought to avenge his own death with the sweet taste of hers. She dared a scamper and got away before his strong hands found purchase on her foot again.

An arrow smashed into his head and half the fight left him. A second hit his throat and rapidly a third went into the side of his chest, just below his extended arm. Lily dared a look at Ray, who readied a fourth arrow to end Powell's cursed undeath. She watched as the arrow left his bow and heard as it hit home, killing the man again.

Sensing something they couldn't, the tree's branch lifted out of his body and left it behind on the ground. Someone would bury the food for it later, once the fires were dealt with.

Lily grabbed more bags of salt as Ray shot another arrow at the two people pursuing Acton and his feverish pyromaniacal trip around the tree. She once again dared a scamper and ran around to the far side of the tree where no salt had been spread. Using her blade she cut two of the bags open at a time, and tossed about their white contents until the bright sun above sparkled everywhere the eye could see. In a minute she had emptied the large bag Powell had carried there, and had spread out all the smaller bags within. All this surrounded by a growing ring of fire under the sky filled with needles large enough to split her in two, and drink everything that fell out dry.

"Run Lily! Get out before it's all aflame," Acton yelled. He turned now, with only a twenty foot gap in the trees not on fire and faced Celine Barber. He pointed behind him towards Ray and Lily ran. She had but a moment before the fires would spread and trap her in with the tree and its thirst for life.

Acton faced the infected woman and made quick work of her old body. He slashed down across her chest and nearly split her in two. The force of the sword's strike sent her to her knees and with a returning backhand slash across at waist height he took her head from her shoulders. Her head had no more than gone still on the ground before the roots of the ravager tree erupted around it, sinking its black, fleshy tendrils into the skin and meat beneath. Acton danced away and slipped through the fires.

Lily, Ray and the captain backed away as the forest took flame, sealing off the tree from its minions should any have survived in the woods. The earth sown with ancestor-imbued and blessed salt as well, the tree would have no choice but to go dormant once again.

"Have we done it?" Ray asked Acton as they watched the fires eat away at the good trees and healthy forest. Another sacrifice made to prevent the spread of the ancient threat.

"I think," Acton said. "But so many dead." He sat on a stone and fished out the waterskin he'd left beside it earlier. He lifted his wet face cloth and drank at it as ravenously as the tree drank blood. Thirst slaked—skin empty—he looked at the boy and girl who came on the dangerous journey. The flicker of fires teased their skin until it glowed with an orange light.

"Powell, Grant, Hadwell and Celine. Several strangers on the road and the entire farm of animals. All dead because of a tree," Lily said, looking at the tree inside the wall of flame. The branches stayed still, somehow knowing again that it had suffered a setback.

"Aye," Acton said. And there'll be more before we're done of it. We'd be lucky if that's all there was. My men and I will scour the forests for days looking for signs of the infected or the risen dead. Elmoryn strikes once more at its curse of humanity."

"We'll come. We'll help," Lily said.

"Such brave ones, you two are. Proper Shire children. Proper Low Marish people. Afraid of nothing," Acton said full of pride.

"Oh we're plenty afraid," Ray said. "I've need of new trousers for the walk back. I never imagined I'd shit myself over fear of a tree."

- About The Author -

CHRIS PHILBROOK is the creator and author of *Adrian's Undead Diary* as well as the fantasy series *Elmoryn* and *Tesser: A Dragon Among Us.*

Chris calls the wonderful state of New Hampshire his home. He is an avid reader, writer, role player, miniatures game player, video game player, and part time athlete, as well as a member of the Horror Writers Association. If you weren't impressed enough, he also works full time while writing for Elmoryn as well as the world of Adrian's Undead Diary, Tesser, and his newest project, *Colony Lost*.

- Find More Online -

Check out Chris Philbrook's official website **thechrisphilbrook.com** to contact the author and keep tabs on his many exciting projects, or follow Chris on Facebook at **www.facebook.com/ChrisPhilbrookAuthor** for special announcements.

Visit **adriansundeaddiary.com** or **elmoryn.com** to access additional content. Learn more about Chris's worlds, contact the author, join discussions with other readers, view maps and concept art from the stories, and receive the latest news about A.U.D. and Elmoryn.

In addition, Chris Philbrook's game development company, Tier One Games LLC, is developing a roleplaying game which allows players to explore the world of Elmoryn, creating their own original characters and adventures. Visit **elmoryn.com** to access the ever-expanding game content as it is released.

Follow Chris Philbrook's latest epic series as it unfolds in *Tesser: A Dragon Among Us*. Meet Tesser, the Dragon. He who walks in any form, and flies the skies free of fear. He has slept for millennia, but now he has awoken in a world ruled by human hands, where science has overshadowed even the glory of old magic. Follow Tesser as he seeks to understand why he slept for so long, and where all the magic has gone. Visit **adragonamongus.com** to learn more.

Can't get enough of AUD?

Visit the School Store at **adriansundeaddiary.com** for stickers, hats, and a wide variety of awesome shirts!

Can't Wait for More?

Look for Chris Philbrook's **FREE** short fiction eBook, *At Least He's Not on Fire.*

Find it on Amazon, Goodreads, or Smashwords today!

Amazon: http://www.amazon.com/dp/B00JSGEKIK

Goodreads: https://www.goodreads.com/book/show/21948978-at-least-he-s-not-on-fire

Smashwords: https://www.smashwords.com/books/view/430970

www.ingramcontent.com/pod-product-compliance
Ingram Content Group UK Ltd.
Pitfield, Milton Keynes, MK11 3LW, UK
UKHW041849190726
13854UKWH00002B/796

9 781523 609420